Once upon a time there was a lovely young boy.
This boy had hopes, dreams and aspirations he hoped one day to achieve.
Though he believed in himself, he hoped to surround himself with those who believed in him too.
Today that boy is a man.

So, for this lovely boy on this milestone day.
Today you find yourself surrounded by those who believed you could, and so you did.
Motivating, inspiring and supporting those around you in the process,
making this world a lovely place to be in.

May you accomplish all you set out to achieve,
Take risks and experience new highs,
Love life and live it to its fullest,
And look forward to the rest of your life,
Happily ever after.

LOVELY
ISBN: 978-0-6484496-7-6

Written by Ben Logan
Illustrated by Amy Curran

Published in Australia by
PINK COFFEE PUBLISHING
PO Box 483, Oberon NSW 2787

Cataloguing-in-Publication entrry is available from the National Library of Australia http://catalogue.nla.gov.au

Lovely

A BEDTIME STORY

THE
MIMS

Once upon a time there was a lovely old house.

It had a lovely old porch, complete with a lovely old door.

And inside that door, a couple lived.

This wasn't your ordinary couple.
This couple had been together for sixty years.
And they never left each others side.

Always waking up at the same time, having breakfast together
and sharing memories of the past and ideas for the future.

But this particular morning was unlike any other.

On this morning, the sweet old man opened his eyes to discover his
beautiful wife was not there.

Not inside the lovely old house, not on the lovely old porch
and not through the lovely old door.

The old man went searching for his wife.

Down the very old steps, to a very old path.

Down the very old path, past a very old cabin.

From the very old cabin, to a very old street.

OLD ST

The old man asked everyone in the street, and in the village,
and no one had seen his wife.

The old man sat down. He didn't know what to do.

He missed his wife so much. She was all he could think about.

He began to walk home.

He walked back down the very old street, past the very old cabin.

From the very old cabin, to the very old path.

From the very old path, to the very old steps.

At the top of the steps, was the lovely old porch, and the lovely old door.

He went through the lovely old door into his lovely old house.

The old man was so sad at the thought of missing his wife.

Suddenly, he heard a strange noise.

It was getting louder and louder, every second.

He searched the whole house and could not find
where it was coming from.

He lay in his bed, eyes wide open. He could still hear the noise.

Then, in the doorway.... a sweet face peering through!

"Wake up deary, it's time for breakfast"

The old man was so delighted to see his wife again.

She had never left him!

Feeling a mixture of sadness and relief, he joined is wife in the kitchen.

They lived the rest of their lives together in
the lovely old house, with the lovely old door,
with a lovely old porch and some lovely old steps.

The End.

www.ingramcontent.com/pod-product-compliance
Lightning Source LLC
Chambersburg PA
CBHW041205100726
47911CB00016B/864